Don Freeman

SCHOLASTIC INC.
New York Toronto London Auckland Sydney
Mexico City New Delhi Hong Kong Buenos Aires

Early one autumn morning, a mother gray squirrel sat talking with her young son, Earl.

"It is high time you went out and learned how to find acorns on your own," she said.

But Earl didn't know the first thing about finding acorns. So away he sailed to visit his friend Jill.

“Good morning, Earl,” said Jill.

"Here is an acorn I've saved for you." Earl was pleased to have found such a big acorn so quickly. His mother would be happy. He twitched and twirled his tail, which was his way of saying, "Thank you very much."

"And here's a nutcracker to help you open it," added Jill.

Earl scampered home, eager to show his mother what he had found. But when she saw him, she said, "Earl, come in here this instant. I want to speak to you!"

"Whoever heard of a squirrel needing a nutcracker? Why, it's absurd," his mother scolded. "You got it from Jill, didn't you? I'll bet she gave you the acorn, too. That girl is making you into the most spoiled squirrel in the world! Now take that nutcracker right back!"

"You're back so quickly! And you didn't want the nutcracker? Well, never mind, I have an extra special present for you!"

And she tied a beautiful red scarf neatly around Earl's furry neck. "I really made it for my doll," she said. "But he wanted you to have it."

How proud Earl was of his scarlet scarf!

Back home he sailed with his tail all unfurled.

But when his mother saw the scarf, she said, "Earl, come in here this instant! I want to speak to you!"

"Whoever heard of any of us needing something around our necks to keep us warm?" his mother fussed.

“Now that girl has done it! You *are* the most spoiled squirrel in the world.”

Earl knew his mother was right. That night after supper, he tied his scarf into the shape of a sack.

While his mother slept, out he crept. Earl wanted to show her that he could find an acorn on his own.

All night long, Earl searched in the bright moonlight, under rocks, up in trees . . .

and inside empty old mole holes, without finding one single solitary acorn anywhere!

By morning, Earl was very tired. In fact, he was all worn out.

His ears were getting cold. He tied the scarf around his head. "That's better!" he said to himself.

Maybe that's an old squirrel hole for me to sleep in . . . thought Earl.

But look who was inside! "Oh, excuse me!" said Earl. "I didn't know you lived in here!"

"Whooo did you think lived here?" hooted the Great Horned Owl loudly. "And whooooever saw a squirrel wearing a scarf?"

“My friend Jill gave it to me,” Earl said proudly. “By the way, could you tell me where I might find an acorn?”

“An acorn?” hooted the Great Horned Owl. “Why, certainly. There’s a giant oak tree right over there full of acorns. But I wouldn’t go anywhere near it if I were a squirrel wearing a scarlet scarf.

"Conrad the bull would not like it one bit. You know what bulls do when they see red? They get awfully mad!"

But Earl didn't hear a word the owl had said about the bull because he was already halfway over to the tree.

And look who was snoozing there so peacefully. Conrad!

Earl hopped up on top of the bull's burly back. He didn't see Conrad's long, sharp horns—all he saw were acorns galore!

“Who’s that tickling my shoulder?” the big bull smoldered.

Earl didn't see Conrad's nose—all he saw was a great way to reach the acorns.

And all Conrad saw was Earl's scarf! Just then . . .

. . . Conrad got awfully mad.

With one flying leap, Earl escaped up into the tree. But his scarf had come untied.

It slipped off his neck, and it dropped.

Quick as a flash, Earl reached down and snatched his scarf. “Don’t you tear my beautiful present!” he shouted.

Conrad snorted and charged with all his might!
He charged right into the tree, and his horns got stuck.

He pulled and yanked until he shook poor Earl out of the tree . . .

. . . along with hundreds of acorns.

BONK! One fell right on top of his head.

ISBN-13: 978-0-439-89569-9
ISBN-10: 0-439-89569-3

Published by Scholastic Inc., 557 Broadway, New York, NY 10012, by arrangement with Viking Children's Books, a member of Penguin Group (USA) Inc.

12 11 10 9 8 7 6 8 9 10 11/0

Printed in the U.S.A. 40

First Scholastic printing, October 2006

Designed by Sam Kim
Set in Cloister